D1491442

LIVING LONG AGO
FOOD AND EATING

Felicity Brooks and Shirley Bond

Edited by Janet Cook and Cheryl Evans

Designed by Chris Scollen

Illustrated by Teri Gower, Guy Smith and Chris Lyon

Series consultant: Dr Anne Millard

Contents

Language adviser: Betty Root M.B.E.

The first food

The first people spent a lot of time hunting animals and gathering food.

Bison

The men did the hunting. They killed animals such as deer, bison, horses, boar and mammoths with wood and stone weapons.

Stone tool

If the animal was big, they chopped it up near to where they killed it. Then they carried the pieces back to their camps.

Learning to cook

People probably first found out that meat tasted better cooked when they dropped it in the fire by mistake. After that they cooked meat on sticks or on flat stones heated up by the fire.

The water was heated up with hot stones.

Hot stones

▲ Before cooking pots were invented, food was boiled in a pit. The pit was lined with skins and filled with water.

They also caught fish from rivers and lakes. The very first people ate their food raw because they had not learned to make fire.

Digging stick

Women collected foods such as berries, bulbs, roots, mushrooms and nuts. They also gathered grubs, eggs and snails.

The first farmers

About 10,000 years ago, people noticed that when seeds were dropped on the ground they grew into plants.

Soon they began to dig the ground especially to plant seeds. These people were the first farmers.

The farmers also began to tame sheep, goats, dogs, pigs and cattle.▼

With these crops and animals, people now had grain, meat and milk. They hunted less as they had more food around them.

Hunting tricks

Hunters used tricks to help them catch animals. Here are some of them.

Disguise

They wore skins so that they could creep up on animals.

Traps

A bison falling into a pit dug by hunters.

They dug deep pits and covered them with sticks. The sticks broke when an animal stepped on them so it fell into the pit.

Fire

They chased animals with burning branches to drive them into swamps and over cliffs.

Animals were afraid of fire and ran away from it.

Sickle

River

They cut the crops with a tool called a sickle made from stone and wood.

Oven for bread

They built houses together near rivers. These were the first villages.

◀ Soon people learned to make cooking pots from clay, weave wool into clothes and make baskets.

◀ By grinding grain they made flour for bread. They baked the bread in dried mud ovens.

Some of these methods are still used in parts of the world.

3

Ancient Egyptian food

The Ancient Egyptians used the flood water from the River Nile to grow their crops. They could usually store enough of this water to last the whole year.

The river flooded every July and soaked the hard ground. The Egyptians dug channels to take the water to the fields.

Wheat was planted in October. By April it was ready to be cut. ▼

Channel

The wheat was cut using a sickle with a flint blade.

Sickle

Men put the wheat in baskets.

Cattle trampled on the wheat to separate the stalks from the grain.

Making bread

This is how the Egyptians made bread. They baked over 40 different kinds.

◀ The grain was ground to make flour.

Flour, water ▶ and salt were mixed to make dough.

◀ Fruit, nuts, garlic or honey might be added.

The dough ▶ was made into loaves and baked.

Oven

Women tossed the grain in the air. This removed its outside covering (chaff).

A scribe counted the baskets.

◀ Grain was stored in granaries. It was used to make bread, beer and cakes.

Grain was poured in here.

Granary

Workers had beer, bread, cheese and onions for lunch. Bread and beer were the main food and drink. ▶

Fishing

Egyptians ate a lot of fish from the Nile such as perch, mullet and eels.

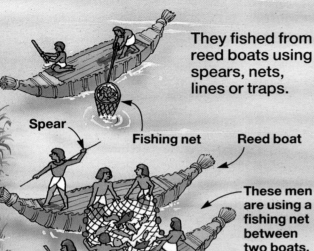

They fished from reed boats using spears, nets, lines or traps.

Spear

Fishing net

Reed boat

These men are using a fishing net between two boats.

Some fish were eaten fresh. Some were dried in the sun or put in jars with salt or oil to stop them going bad.

Hunting wild ducks with a throwing stick.

Bow and arrow

◀ They also hunted wild birds such as geese, ducks and storks. They hunted for sport as well as for food.

Tombs

The pictures and writing on the walls of Ancient Egyptian tombs tell us a lot about what they ate. They show people farming, shopping, cooking, baking and eating.

The Egyptians believed people had another life after they were dead. They put food and other useful things in a tomb when a person was buried. These were for the person to use in his next life.

Egyptian meals

Rich Egyptians ate many of the same things that we can buy today. Here are some of them.

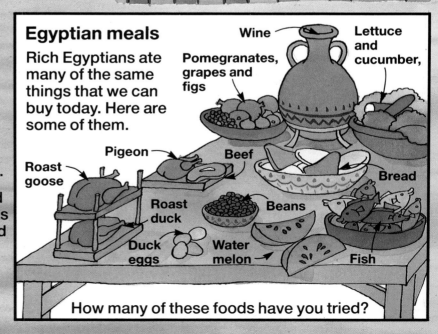

Wine

Lettuce and cucumber,

Pomegranates, grapes and figs

Pigeon

Beef

Roast goose

Bread

Roast duck

Beans

Duck eggs

Water melon

Fish

How many of these foods have you tried?

Roman food

The Romans came from Italy. The poor people who lived there ate mostly bread and a kind of porridge made from wheat.

Only rich people could afford meat, fish, cheese and vegetables. They ate very well and often had big dinner parties.

Preparing for a party

In rich houses, slaves spent all day preparing the food. Kitchens were hot and smoky because food was cooked on open fires.

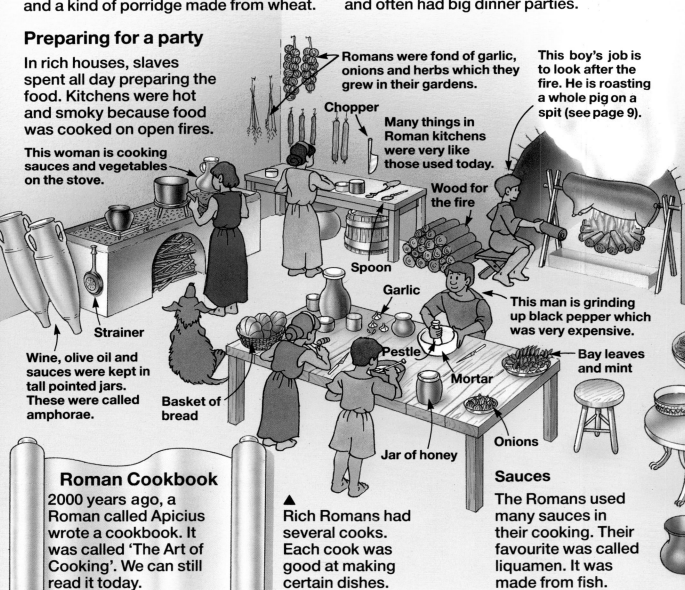

Romans were fond of garlic, onions and herbs which they grew in their gardens.

Chopper

Many things in Roman kitchens were very like those used today.

This boy's job is to look after the fire. He is roasting a whole pig on a spit (see page 9).

This woman is cooking sauces and vegetables on the stove.

Wood for the fire

Spoon

Strainer

Garlic

This man is grinding up black pepper which was very expensive.

Wine, olive oil and sauces were kept in tall pointed jars. These were called amphorae.

Basket of bread

Pestle

Mortar

Bay leaves and mint

Jar of honey

Onions

Roman Cookbook

2000 years ago, a Roman called Apicius wrote a cookbook. It was called 'The Art of Cooking'. We can still read it today.

▲ Rich Romans had several cooks. Each cook was good at making certain dishes.

Sauces

The Romans used many sauces in their cooking. Their favourite was called liquamen. It was made from fish.

A Roman recipe

This is how you can make a Roman bread pudding.

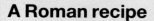

You will need:
1½ thick slices of bread,
300 ml (½ pint) milk,
150 ml (¼ pint) olive oil,
Honey

1. Cut the ▶
bread into
fairly large
pieces.

◀ 2. Soak the
pieces in
the milk.

3. Fry them in
hot oil.* Drain
on paper
towels. Serve
with honey.

Good manners

After eating, it was polite to burp to show you had enjoyed the meal. Guests often brought napkins to take home filled with food to eat later.

Get an adult to help you with this.

A dinner party

Parties started late in the afternoon and lasted many hours. Slaves brought the food from the kitchen.

There were three couches in the dining room arranged around the table. People ate lying down.

Romans drank wine mixed with water. Sometimes honey was also added.

People ate with their fingers. Sometimes they used spoons. There were no forks.

Red mullet

Lobster

Roast peacock

Chicken

Bread

Boar's head

Bowl of water

There were three courses for a dinner. These people are eating a main course.

Guests washed their fingers after each course.

First course

Eggs

Stuffed dormice

Bread

Salad

Oysters and mushrooms

Snails

Dessert

Honey cakes

Stuffed dates

Nuts

Fruit

Fruit tarts

What the Vikings ate

The Vikings came from Sweden, Denmark and Norway. The weather there was cold and snowy in winter and the summers were short. Viking farmers had to work very hard to grow and store enough food to last through the long winter.

They grew barley, wheat, oats and rye to make into bread, porridge and beer.

In their small vegetable gardens they grew peas, onions and cabbages.

Cows, chickens, sheep, pigs and geese were kept for meat, milk and eggs.

The Vikings caught a lot of fish and hunted seals with spears.

They also caught sea-birds with nets and collected their eggs to eat.

Viking hunters killed wild animals such as boar and deer with bows and arrows.

Keeping food

The Vikings salted or dried a lot of meat and fish. This stopped it from going bad.

Meat was ▶ dried above a fire. Fish were dried in the sun.

Cutting up meat

◀ Pieces of meat were put in barrels with salt made from seawater.

Salt

Bread made from rye flour and oatcakes were baked on hot stones by the fire. ▶

Bread

Drinking cup made from cow horn

Beer

8

Viking meals

Vikings had two main meals a day at about eight in the morning and seven in the evening. They cooked, ate and slept in the one large room of their houses.

Barrels of cheese and sour milk

Beer

They ate with their fingers, knives and spoons.

Barrel of mead (honey drink)

Rye bread

Beef

Wild boar

Apples

Wooden plate

Eggs

Cabbage

Linen table-cloth

Peas

Bowls carved out of soapstone

Caul-dron

Spit

Big fire in the centre of the room

Food was cooked on iron poles called spits or in large metal pots called cauldrons over a fire.

Make a toy cauldron*

You will need a small hollow ball (about the size of a tennis ball), three sticks 8ins long, a piece of wire 8ins long, some aluminum foil, some string, a paper-clip, a skewer and a sharp knife.

1 Cut the ball in half.** Cover one half with foil.

2 Make holes on either side of this half ball.**

3 Put ends of the wire in the holes and bend them up.

4 Tie the sticks with the string to make a tripod.

5 Hook the cauldron to the string with the paper-clip.

*DO NOT try to light a fire under your cauldron.
** Get an adult to help you.

9

Medieval food

In medieval times, many people in Europe were poor farmers. They lived in small villages belonging to a lord. They had to work very hard for the lord and ate the same food almost every day.

Life in a village

Each village had three big fields. Every family had strips of land in each field. There they grew wheat and rye for bread, barley for beer, and oats.

They also kept animals for milk, meat and eggs and grew vegetables in small vegetable gardens.

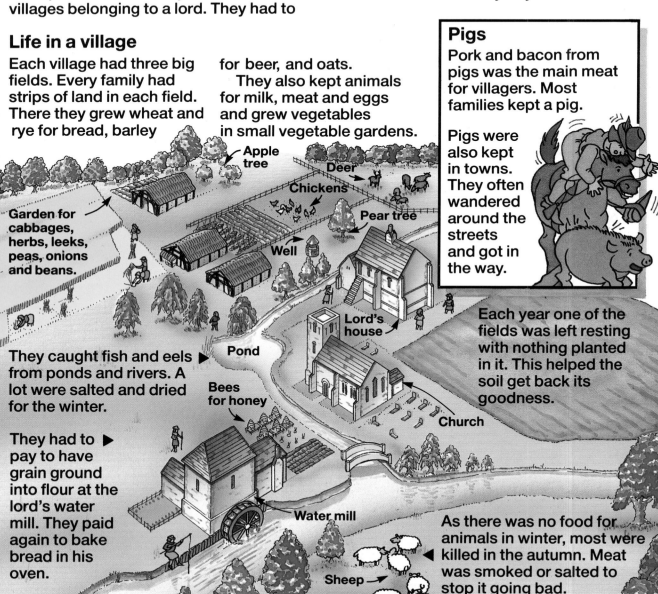

Pigs

Pork and bacon from pigs was the main meat for villagers. Most families kept a pig.

Pigs were also kept in towns. They often wandered around the streets and got in the way.

Apple tree

Deer

Chickens

Pear tree

Garden for cabbages, herbs, leeks, peas, onions and beans.

Well

Lord's house

Pond

Each year one of the fields was left resting with nothing planted in it. This helped the soil get back its goodness.

They caught fish and eels ▶ from ponds and rivers. A lot were salted and dried for the winter.

Bees for honey

Church

They had to ▶ pay to have grain ground into flour at the lord's water mill. They paid again to bake bread in his oven.

Water mill

As there was no food for animals in winter, most were killed in the autumn. Meat was smoked or salted to stop it going bad.

Sheep ➤

10

Meals

For breakfast villagers had bread and watery beer (ale). Beer was their usual drink. For lunch they had the same, maybe with cheese and an onion.

In the evening they had thick soup (pottage) made from things such as pork, onions, cabbage, beans, oats and water.

Soup was made in a pot above the fire. The pot was emptied out only once a year before Lent (see Church days).

Each day more food was added to the leftovers.

Pease puddings

Dumplings were also cooked inside the pot. Some were made from rye flour, others from dried peas and beans. These were called pease puddings. They were tied in a cloth and hung in the pot.

Food around the world

These are some of the things people ate at this time around the world.

Bread, cabbage, beans, salted pork, cheese, soup.

Rice, pork, vegetables.

North America

Europe

Corn, deer, beans, fish, bison, turkey.

Corn pancakes, tomatoes, potatoes, peppers, beans.

South America

Africa

India China

N

Millet porridge, beans, milk, beef.

Rice, vegetables and a spicy sauce.

Australia

Church days

It was a Christian church rule that nobody must eat meat on Fridays or in Lent (40 days before Easter). During this time they ate a lot of salted fish.

The only time they ate well and did not work was on Christmas Day and a few other holidays.

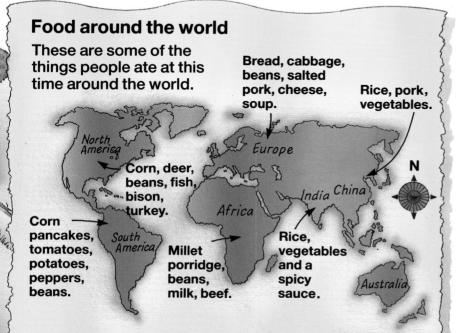

Dancing on May Day.

Medieval banquets

In medieval times rich families lived in big houses or castles. They had cooks to make many different kinds of food. They often invited guests to a banquet.

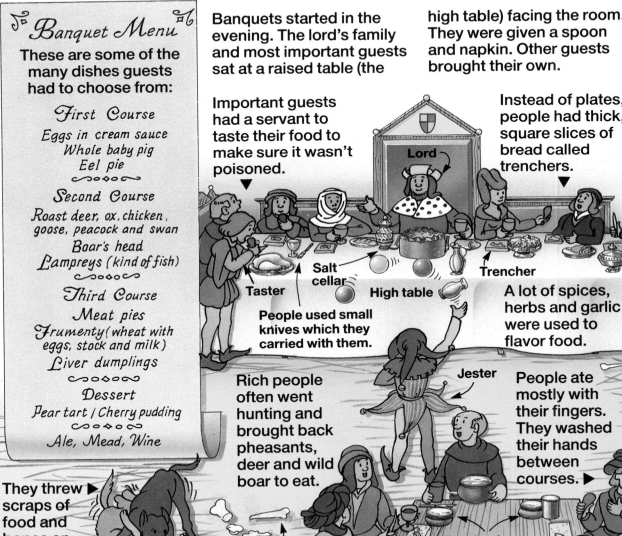

♫ Banquet Menu ♫

These are some of the many dishes guests had to choose from:

First Course
Eggs in cream sauce
Whole baby pig
Eel pie
∽∘◇∘∾

Second Course
Roast deer, ox, chicken, goose, peacock and swan
Boar's head
Lampreys (kind of fish)
∽∘◇∘∾

Third Course
Meat pies
Frumenty (wheat with eggs, stock and milk)
Liver dumplings
∽∘◇∘∾

Dessert
Pear tart / Cherry pudding
∽∘◇∘∾
Ale, Mead, Wine

Banquets started in the evening. The lord's family and most important guests sat at a raised table (the high table) facing the room. They were given a spoon and napkin. Other guests brought their own.

Important guests had a servant to taste their food to make sure it wasn't poisoned. ▼

Instead of plates, people had thick, square slices of bread called trenchers. ▼

Lord

Salt cellar

Taster

High table

Trencher

People used small knives which they carried with them.

A lot of spices, herbs and garlic were used to flavor food.

Rich people often went hunting and brought back pheasants, deer and wild boar to eat.

Jester

People ate mostly with their fingers. They washed their hands between courses. ▶

They threw ▶ scraps of food and bones on the floor for the dogs.

Bones for the dogs

Bowls of mustard and spices

How to make medieval fish pasties

You will need:

½ cup butter,
1 small onion, finely chopped,
1½ lbs smoked fish (mackerel, trout or eel),
1 egg, beaten,
6 eggs, hard boiled and chopped,
½ teaspoon each of salt, pepper, mace and ginger,
1 package pie crust.

1 Set oven to Gas Mark 4*. In a pan, fry the onion in the butter.

2 Remove bones from fish. Flake it with fork. Add onion.

3 Add spices, pepper, salt and chopped eggs. Roll out pastry.

4 Cut out 4in circles. Put some mixture in the middle of each one.

5 Wet edges of circles with water. Fold pastry over. Pinch edges.

6 Put on oiled baking tray. Brush with egg. Bake for 25 minutes.

Musicians played for the guests while they were eating.

◀ Sometimes a cook roasted a peacock or swan. He sewed its feathers and skin back on before it was served.

Small birds

Salted fish

Fish pasties

Most guests shared a dish of food with another guest. ▼

Surprise pies

A cook sometimes made a big empty pie. As a joke, after it was cooked, he put small live birds into the pie through a hole in the bottom. When the pie was cut, the birds flew out, surprising the guests.

Can you see a surprise pie in the main picture?

*Electric 180°C or 350°F.

13

Discovering different foods

About 500 years ago, European sailors began to explore the world. They found many countries which they had not known about before. They also found a lot of new foods. They brought some of these back to Europe.

New foods for Europe

These are some of the new foods that travellers brought to Europe.

Artichokes from Peru

Corn from South America

Tomatoes from South America

Early tomatoes ▲ were yellow and knobbly. They were called 'golden apples'.

Turkeys from Mexico

Peanuts from South America

Peppers

Cauliflowers

People did not like some new foods at first. It was 200 years before ▶ potatoes were very popular.

Potatoes from Peru

The search for spices

Cinnamon
Pepper
Nutmeg
Ginger

At this time, a lot of spices were used to flavor food, especially meat that was going bad.

These spices were brought to Europe across land by Arab traders. They were very expensive.

As they sailed, they found countries such as North and South America. They called them the New World.

INDIA
SRI LANKA
EAST INDIES

The spices came from countries in the East, such as India, the East Indies and Sri Lanka.

The European sailors began to look for a way to the East to bring back the spices by sea.

They often just took what they wanted and treated the people living there very badly or killed them.

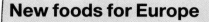

14

In the kitchen

Cooking was still done over an open fire. In a rich home they ate a lot of meat. This was cooked on a spit. Bread and pies were cooked in a separate oven.

Bread oven

Metal cauldrons hanging above the fire were used for cooking soups and stews.

Smoked meats

Pans to catch fat

Sugar was sold in lumps. It was cut up with sugar cutters.

Sugar cutters

Sugar

Spice box

Store cupboard

Jug of beer

Basket of vegetables

Sailors' food

Sailors spent weeks at sea. They had little fresh water and no way of storing fresh food. The food they took often went bad.

Dry cheese

Salted fish and meat

Biscuits (often full of worms)

Beer

They sometimes ate sea-birds, sharks and rats.

Scurvy

Many sailors died of a disease called scurvy. This was because they had no fresh fruit or vegetables.

The rich had metal plates. Others had wooden ones.

Aztec food

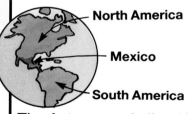

North America

Mexico

South America

The Aztec people lived in Mexico. In 1521, Spanish sailors came seeking gold. They conquered the Aztecs.

The sailors had never seen many of these foods before.

Aztecs ate corn porridge and pancakes (tortillas), tomatoes, peppers, beans, turkey and chocolate.

The sailors liked some Aztec foods and brought them back to Europe.

The Aztecs also ate dogs and sometimes frogs, tadpoles, newts, worms, flies, ants, and lizards.

Food in the New World

People from Europe began to travel to the New World (North and South America) to start new lives there.

The story of Thanksgiving

In 1620, a group of people sailed from England to the east coast of America. They landed on 10th November.

It was too late in the year and too cold to plant the rye and wheat seeds they had brought with them.

The Indians who lived there gave them food. Even so, only half the English people survived the hard winter.

In the spring, the Indians taught them how to grow corn and beans and to hunt. Their next harvest was good.

Corn flour bread

They made a feast of turkey and other foods to celebrate. They invited the Indians who had helped them.

Americans still celebrate this harvest on Thanksgiving day. They have a meal of turkey and pumpkin pie.

Pumpkin pie*

You will need:

¼ cup butter,
2 lbs pumpkin, peeled and sliced,
3 apples, peeled, cored and sliced,
½ lb sultanas,
1 lb pie dough,
3 eggs, beaten,
1 cup cream,
1 cup brown sugar,
½ teaspoon each of ground ginger, cinnamon, nutmeg, cloves and allspice.

1
Fry the pumpkin in the butter on a low heat until light brown. Keep the juice that is made.

2
Put the pumpkin pieces into a bowl over a pan of boiling water. Cook until just soft.

This is how pumpkin pie was made over 300 years ago.

3

In another pan, stew the apples and sultanas in the pumpkin juice until they are just soft.

4

Roll out the pastry and line a 9in flan dish. Put a layer of apples and sultanas in it.

5

Add the beaten eggs to the pumpkin. Mix in the cream, sugar and spices. Pour into the flan dish.

6

Cook the pie at Gas Mark 6* for 10 minutes, then at Mark 4** for 20-25 minutes. Serve hot.

New drinks in Europe

390 years ago tea, coffee and chocolate were brought to Europe for the first time. Coffee houses opened where people could buy these new drinks and talk to their friends.

In many cities in Europe, such as Paris and Vienna, a lot of coffee houses later became cafés.

Chocolate

Chocolate was brought to Europe from South America and the West Indies. At first it was always made into a drink, no one ate it. ▶

Tea

Tea has been drunk in China for about 1,300 years. It was first brought to Europe in 1610.

China cup

Tea soon became a popular drink, especially in England. ▶

Coffee

Coffee first grew in Africa. It was later brought to Europe from Turkey. ▶

A coffee house

Samuel Pepys
Samuel Pepys lived in London over 300 years ago. He wrote a diary which tells us about the food he ate. This is what he gave his guests for dinner in 1663.

Rabbit and chicken stew
A leg of mutton
Three carps (fish)
A side of lamb
A dish of roasted pigeons
Four lobsters
Three tarts
Lamprey (fish) pie
A dish of anchovies
Good wine

*Electric 400°F or 200°C.   **Electric 350°F or 180°C.

Better food in Europe

About 230 years ago farmers began to look for new ways of growing food and breeding animals to eat.

This meant that the rich people had better food. Poor people still had very little choice of food.

A meal in a town house

Rich families, like this one, ate their main meal at about six or seven o'clock in the evening.

Poor people often had to beg for food.

Sugar

Sugar came from large farms, called sugar plantations, in places such as South America and the West Indies. People from Africa were captured and forced to work as slaves on the farms.

Table manners

In 1788, an English book called 'The Honours of the Table' told guests how to behave while they were eating. It said you must not:

◀ Scratch any part of your body or pick your teeth.

◀ Blow your nose or spit, or sit too far from the table.

If you needed to go to the rest room, you were supposed to creep out without anybody noticing. When you came back, you could not say where you had been.

Because sugar ▶ was much cheaper than before, there were many different kinds of sweet cakes and puddings.

People began to eat fruit raw instead of always cooked.

Forks

400 years ago people began using forks in Italy. Over the following 100 years, forks started to be used in the rest of Europe.

Early forks only had two prongs.

Fork with three prongs from 200 years ago

Gardens

Gardeners had better seeds, so they began to grow better kinds of fruit and vegetables.

The first sandwich

One day in 1760, John Montague, Earl of Sandwich played cards for 24 hours non-stop.

He asked for his meat to be put between two pieces of bread so that he could eat and carry on playing. This was the first sandwich.

◀ Rich people had beautiful plates and dishes made of china or silver.

Meat

Farmers had new foods which kept animals alive over the winter, so there was more fresh meat.

Potato pie

Potatoes were now used in many different recipes. This potato pie makes a lunch for six people.

You will need:

3 lbs potatoes, peeled or scrubbed,
2 large carrots, finely grated,
Juice of 2 oranges,
½ cup butter
2 eggs,
1 teaspoon sugar,
Salt and pepper,
1 cup grated cheese

1 Set the oven to Gas Mark 4 (Electric 180°C, 350°F) ▶

2 Boil the potatoes until soft. ◀ Mash them.

Add all other ingredients. Beat them into potato. ▶

3

4 Put mixture into a dish. Bake for 20 minutes. ◀ Serve hot.

Eating too much

Rich men often ate too much meat and too many cakes, pies and sweet things. They also drank far too much alcohol.

They often got a painful disease called gout. This made their fingers and toes swell up.

French cooks

About 300 years ago French cooks first became famous for their good cooking.

Cooks wrote recipe books which became very popular.

The most famous cook was Antoinin Carême. He was called 'the cook of kings and the king of cooks'.

Ships

Different countries around the world grew different kinds of food. Many of these were brought to Europe in sailing ships.

Kitchen inventions

Inventions such as cooking ranges, gas ovens, ice boxes and cans made cooking and storing food much easier. For a long time, however, these things were too expensive for poor people to buy. They still ate simple food which they cooked over an open fire as they had done for thousands of years.

Canned food

In 1813, food was sealed in cans for the first time. To start with, cans were used mainly by sailors as the food kept for a long time. By 1880, cans were very popular.

A can from 1880

An early can opener

Canned food could be sent all over the world. A lot was sent to Europe from Australia.

Cooking ranges

Some people could ▶ afford the new kind of ovens made from iron. These were called cooking ranges.

They were heated by a coal or wood fire. Many could heat hot water too.

Coal fire   Oven

The ashes had to be cleaned from the grate every day.

Gas cookers

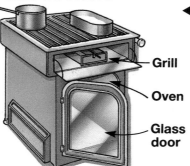

Grill

Oven

Glass door

◀ Gas cookers were invented in 1802, but most homes didn't have one for another 100 years.

Gas cookers were clean and easy to use but, like ranges, they didn't have a temperature control. You judged the heat of the oven by putting your hand inside.

Factories

Some food was now made in factories by machines, instead of being made by hand at home.

Machine for mixing dough for bread from 1880

Ice Boxes

You had to put a ▶ big block of ice inside the first ice boxes. This kept the food cold.

This wooden ice box was made in America in 1874.

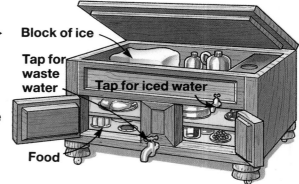

Block of ice

Tap for waste water

Tap for iced water

Food

Factory workers' food

The people who went to towns to work in factories had little money and poor food. The only hot meal many of them got was free soup from soup kitchens.

Soup kitchen in 1851

A factory worker's day.
5 a.m. Get up.
6–8 a.m. Work.
Breakfast – tea or coffee and bread.
Back to work until 12pm.
Lunch – potatoes with lard, sometimes a little bacon.
1 p.m. – 7 p.m. work.
Supper – tea or beer, potatoes or porridge, bread, perhaps a little meat.

Potato disease

In 1845, potatoes all over Europe started rotting in the fields because of a disease called blight.

Potatoes were the main food for a lot of poor people.

Poor people starved because they had nothing else to eat. In Ireland, thousands died. Many left to go to other countries such as America.

Fold a party napkin

Try this with a large paper or linen napkin.

1. Fold the napkin in three lengthways.

2. Fold the ends to meet in the middle.

3. Fold down top corners and turn the napkin over.

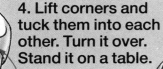

4. Lift corners and tuck them into each other. Turn it over. Stand it on a table.

Rich people's food

As always, rich people could afford many different kinds of food. They had servants to buy, cook and serve their meals. They often had dinner parties with seven or more courses.

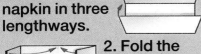

A dinner party 100 years ago

Rich people had beautiful china and many kinds of knives, forks, spoons and glasses.

Changes everywhere

The way food is grown, prepared, sold, cooked and eaten has changed a lot in the last 100 years. Electricity, for example, has made a big difference on farms and in factories as well as in kitchens.

The first electric cooker was made in 1895, but to start with most people could not afford new electrical things. Below you can see some of the things people with enough money could buy by about 1930.

Shopping

Until about 40 years ago there were no supermarkets. People had to go to several shops to buy different things. Food was not usually sold in packages. The shopkeeper weighed and packed the amount you wanted.

1930s Electric kitchen

Early dishwashers looked like this. The first was made in 1899. ▼

A few homes now had electric ice boxes to keep food fresh.

Dishwasher

Electric kettle

Refrigerator

Some kinds of food were sold in packages.

Electric and gas cookers were cleaner and safer than fires. The first cooker with a temperature control was made in 1933.

Pickled onions

Dried raisins

People still ▶ smoked, dried or pickled food to stop it going bad.

Smoked fish

More food could now be bought in cans.

Rationing

During the Second World War (1939-1945) food was short, so in some countries it was rationed. This meant each person could only have a small amount of certain foods each week.

9oz sugar

2oz coffee

47½oz milk

1½oz jam

A little meat

3½oz cheese

½ egg

9oz fat

A ration book showed what each person could have.

RATION BOOK

Using machines

In the past people grew all their own food and did everything by hand. Now most food comes from large farms. It is often prepared and put in packages by machines. This, for example, is how bread is made from wheat today.

Wheat is ▶ grown on a farm and cut down by a machine called a combine harvester.

Combine harvester

The wheat is ▶ ground into flour by machines in a big factory.

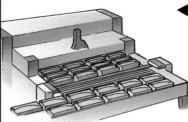

◀ Bread is baked, sliced and packed in a bakery. This oven bakes 2,400 loaves an hour.

Look at page 4 to see how Ancient Egyptians made bread 5000 years ago.

Early electric toasters had to be plugged into a cooker. The first was made in 1909.

Toaster

Bread

▲ Sliced bread could be bought by 1930, but most people cut up their bread at home.

Restaurants

The idea of eating out started in France in 1765. Restaurants have only become popular in other places in the last 100 years.

Many modern restaurants serve food from other countries.

At take-out restaurants you can buy meals to take home.

No change

Some people in the world still hunt, fish and gather food or grow the food they need.

People in the Kalahari desert in Botswana use bows and arrows for hunting.

Many people in the world still don't get enough to eat. Some aid groups try to help by looking for better ways to grow and share food.

Index

First published in 1989 by
Usborne Publishing Ltd,
Usborne House,
83-85 Saffron Hill,
London EC1N 8RT.
© 1989 Usborne Publishing Ltd.

Printed in Belgium.

American edition 1989